HOOEY HIGGINS
and the
Storm

For Jane Rait, with love
S.V.

For Hattie Lefkir, with love
E.D.

HOOEY HIGGINS
and the
Storm

STEVE VOAKE
illustrated by Emma Dodson

WALKER
BOOKS

First published 2014 by Walker Books Ltd
87 Vauxhall Walk, London SE11 5HJ

2 4 6 8 10 9 7 5 3 1

Text © 2014 Steve Voake
Illustrations © 2014 Emma Dodson

The right of Steve Voake and Emma Dodson to be identified as
author and illustrator respectively of this work has been asserted by
them in accordance with the Copyright, Designs and Patents Act 1988

This book has been typeset in StempelSchneidler and EDodson

Printed and bound in Great Britain
by Clays Ltd, St Ives plc

British Library Cataloguing in Publication Data:
a catalogue record for this book is available from the British Library

ISBN 978-1-4063-4331-1

www.walker.co.uk

CONTENTS

Ricky Mears

Samantha

Wayne
Burkett

Yasmin
Boothroyd

Bertie
Milsom

STORMY SKIES

"I hate wet playtimes," said Twig, taking out a packet of Monster Munch. "All we do is sit and watch the same DVDs we've seen a gazillion times."

"You don't *have* to watch them," said Hooey. "You could read a book. Teach yourself some facts."

"I already know loads of facts."

"OK, give me one."

Twig stared at his packet of crisps.

"Not a Monster Munch, Twig. A fact."

"Right, gotcha. Ummm ... there are more calories in a single packet of Monster Munch than there are in a fully grown elephant."

"That's not true, though, is it?"

"Might be."

"But it isn't."

"How do you know?"

"It's called having a brain, Twig. Funnily enough, I just had a text from yours."

"Ooh, what did it say?"

"It said it's still where you left it in *Dunkin' Donuts* and please could you come and pick it up right away."

"**Oh, ha ha,**" said Twig.

"For your information, I actually know loads of stuff. Go on, ask me something."

"All right. Who was Florence Nightingale?"

"Ooh, I know this one. Does he play football for Man United?"

"It's a *she*, Twig. Florence Nightingale was a *woman*."

"OK, Woman United."

"Twig, a) there's no such team and b) she wasn't a footballer, she was a nurse."

"So why was she playing football?"

Hooey sighed.

"Maybe we should just watch the film," he said.

"No, go on, ask me another. One that isn't about football this time."

11

"Right, OK, here goes: what is the capital of England? Is it: a) Cheddar, b) Cheese, or c) the big well-known capital city of London, which isn't in France or Scotland?"

"I do know this," said Twig. "Is it Wolverhampton?"

"Near enough," said Hooey.

"Get *in*!" said Twig, clenching his fist and pulling it down in front of his face. "SCORE!"

He tipped the last bits of Monster Munch into his mouth and then began rummaging around in his lunchbox.

"All this thinking's made me hungry," he said, taking out three bars of chocolate, two digestives and a pork pie. "Time for a teensy bit of tiffin."

Hooey pointed to a few wilted leaves at the bottom of the lunchbox.

"What's that?"

"That," whispered Twig, "is my salad." He unwrapped a Snickers Bar and glanced at Samantha as she walked over. "I'm watching my weight."

"Hi, losers," said Samantha. "What's going on?"

"We've been playing hunt the brain cell," said Hooey. "Think it must have blown away."

"Well, if it hasn't, it will later," said Samantha.

There's going to be a big storm.

"Like the one in my heart," said Twig, picking up Yasmin's magazine and reading from his horoscope. "Listen to this:

> **Your natural charm will bring good luck to someone special and maybe even a touch of romance. Life will be sweet."**

"I mean, hello, people. Sound stormy enough for ya?"

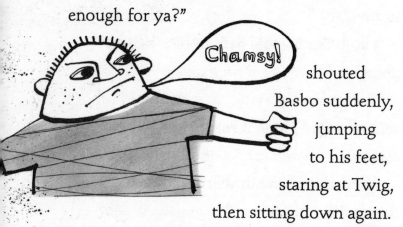

"Chamsy!" shouted Basbo suddenly, jumping to his feet, staring at Twig, then sitting down again.

"That was weird," said Twig.

"This storm in your heart," said Samantha. "Is it three hundred miles across and spinning like a tumble drier?"

Twig placed a hand on his chest and frowned. "I don't *think* so."

"Then not the same," said Samantha. "This storm is sweeping towards Shrimpton at over one hundred miles an hour."

"One hundred miles an hour!" cried Twig. "Let's get prepared! We need to go and get stuff!"

"Like what?" asked Hooey.

"Give me a minute," said Twig. "It's got something to do with wet weather. And ... something to do with clothing. I've got it! Wet weather clothing!"

Samantha looked at Hooey.

"Good luck with the brain-cell hunt," she said. "I'm going to watch the news."

"She's so clever," said Twig, carefully tearing his horoscope out of the magazine and putting it in his pocket. "I bet she even knows what team Florence Nightingale plays for."

"**Oi!**" shouted Wayne as Samantha picked up the remote and changed the picture from *Happy Feet* to the lunchtime news. "I was watching that!"

"You can see dancing penguins anytime," said Samantha. "But this is real life."

"So are dancing penguins," said Wayne. He turned to Ricky with a worried look on his face. "They are, aren't they?"

Before Ricky could answer, a man in a grey suit appeared on the screen and pointed to a weather map.

"At the moment the storm is out in the Atlantic," he said, "but we expect it to arrive on the south coast later this afternoon. The Met Office has issued a Severe Weather Warning for the whole area."

So please be warned: it's going to be very wet and windy out there over the next twenty four hours.

Basbo sat in the corner and thumped the side of his head.

Needle-ucky chamsy,

he muttered. "Needle-ucky chamsy, Needle-ucky chamsy, needle-ucky cham."

"What's he banging on about?" asked Twig.

Basbo leapt to his feet, pushed his desk out of the way and pointed at Twig.

"Bazzer not bangin'! Twigsit get fwapped if he dunt gerralucky chamfer Bazzer!"

Twig looked at Samantha.

Translation?

"He says he wants a lucky charm," explained Samantha. "And he wants you to get it for him."

"Lucky me," said Twig. "What's he want a lucky charm for?"

"Probably to do with that picture of his dad in the paper," said Samantha.

Twig frowned. "The one where he ran over a police car in his cement mixer?"

"No, the one after the storm, remember? It was a few years back."

"Oh, I remember that," said Hooey. "He was standing by a fallen tree and the headline was: **BUILDER SAVED BY LUCKY CHARM.**"

"That's the one," said Samantha. "He was wearing a rabbit's foot around his neck."

"**Ee-yeww, gross,**" said Twig.
"I'm not chopping off some bunny's foot just
to save Basbo from a bit of wind."

"He should try Rennies," said Wayne,
"that's what my auntie uses. Don't think
they work, though."

"**Needle-ucky chamsy!**" shouted
Basbo again, thumping the desk. "**Needle-
ucky cham!**"

"I think I read the wrong horoscope,"

said Twig.

Wayne grabbed the
remote back and soon
everyone was watching
dancing penguins again.

"Are you thinking what I'm thinking?"
asked Hooey.

"I am," said Twig. "But where are we
going to get a dancing penguin at this time
of day?"

"I wasn't thinking about penguins," said Hooey.

I was thinking that we need to find Will and make a plan.

Twig nodded. "I was also thinking that," he said.

FANTASTIC FAN

"Thanks for coming early," said Hooey as he opened the door to Twig. "Will needs our help with something before school starts."

"Your Will's an actual genius," said Twig as they climbed the stairs to the attic. "Last summer my nan had a problem with carrot flies and he solved it just like that."

"How?"

"Told her to stop planting carrots."

"Wow."

"I know. Awesome."

Hooey stopped on the landing and gazed out of the window.

There's definitely a storm coming,

: he said.

Twig nodded. "What's out there, it reminds me of that advert."

"Which one?"

"Sky."

When they reached the attic, Will was standing next to a giant fan with a clipboard in his hand.

"Here she is," he said, tapping the fan with his pencil. "All set up and ready to go."

"Farmer Jenkins has got a fan like that," said Twig. "He uses it to stop his sheds from overheating."

"Same one," said Will. "I showed him how to rig up his scarecrow with an old tape recorder that shouts, *"Get off my land!"* and he was so pleased, he let me borrow his fan."

He ran his pencil across the fan's protective cage and it made a **brrrring** sound.

"That is one massive fan," said Hooey admiringly. "But wouldn't it be easier just to turn the heating down? Or open a window or something?"

"It's not for cooling things down," said Will. "It's for testing out my **Wet and Windy Weather Gear.**"

"Storms make me hungry," said Twig, pushing Maltesers into his mouth and offering the bag to Hooey. Hooey took one.

"Are you going to try and make it stormy in here, then, Will?"

That's the plan,

said Will.

"The fan plan," said Twig, although it sounded more like, "Va fom pom," because of the Maltesers.

"It's not finished yet," said Will, unrolling a sheet of wallpaper. "But these drawings should give you some idea."

The first one showed
a pair of wellies, beside
which Will had written
GRAVITY BOOTS.

The next was a picture of a
pointy hat labelled WILL'S
WIND-CUTTING WIMPLE.

Then there was
a pair of trousers
with sharp creases
down the legs.
BREEZE-SLICERS
was written underneath.

Finally, there was
a jacket which said:
FLOAT COAT.

"All I need to do now," said Will, "is test them."

He looked at Hooey.

Hooey nodded and smiled.

"I guess it would require someone really brave and intelligent to test them out," he said. "Someone who wouldn't mind being thought of as a hero when people found out that he'd done such an incredible and amazing thing."

"Ooh," said Twig, thrusting his hand in the air. "Ooh, ooh."

"I know what you mean, Hooey," said Will. "But who do we know with those kind of qualities?"

"I'll do it!" cried Twig. "Pick me, pick me!"

Hooey grinned. "Now why didn't we think of that?" he said.

28

Will reached under the bed and pulled out a flat piece of wood. It was mounted on rollerskates and slid smoothly into the middle of the room. Carefully laid out on top was Will's Wet and Windy Weather Gear.

"Oh, look!" squealed Twig, hopping from foot to foot. "I'll be like Batman and you'll be like Alfred the Butler, all quiet and brainy and giving me loads of crime-fighty stuff and that."

"It's not about fighting crime," said Will, "it's about not getting blown over."

"Even so," said Twig, clapping his hands.

Dressing up!

He picked
up the trousers
and Hooey saw that they
were a pair of Grandpa's
old brown slacks. Will had
sewn cardboard flaps
into the legs so that the creases
stuck out like sharp blades.

"I call these my Breeze-Slicers,"
said Will. "They'll cut through air like a
shark through water. When you put these
on, the wind will run right around you and
blow next door's fence down instead."

"It'll be like a film," said Twig. "About

fences blowing down
and stuff. And also that
Twister one where a

cow flies through the air and goes
Moooooooooo-smack."

"That's how *everyone* should get their

milk delivered," said
Hooey. "Imagine a cow
landing on your doorstep
every morning. That'd
certainly wake you up."

"You'd probably get some
yogurt as well," said Will. "What with
all the spinning around."

"Or butter," said
Hooey. "Some sort of
dairy product, anyway."

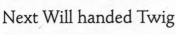

Next Will handed Twig
what appeared to be a silver wizard's hat
with a bungee cord attached.

31

"**Oh, hello!**" said Twig. "Is this a magical crime-fighting helmet I see before me? I think it is!"

"Or a traffic cone covered in Baco-Foil," said Hooey.

"Actually neither," said Will. "**It's a Wind-Cutting Wimple.** Built by my own fair hand."

Twig put it on his head and watched it slowly sink over his face.

"**It's a bit dark in here,**" he said.

Hooey lifted the wimple back onto the top of Twig's head and stuffed a sock in each side.

"Is that better?"

Twig stared at himself in the mirror. "Now I

look like a dog who's got his head stuck in a traffic cone."

"Don't knock it," said Hooey, stretching out the bungee cord and snapping it beneath Twig's chin. "They'll all be wearing these next year."

"Tilt your head forward," said Will.

Twig pointed his head at the floor.

"Not that far," said Will.

Twig pointed his head at the ceiling.

"Now you look like a unicorn who's just been shot," said Hooey. "Or been given some very bad news."

"Like being told he has to wear a traffic cone on his head," said Twig.

"It's not a traffic cone, it's a wimple," said Will.

He reached down to the
trolley and took
a yellow oilskin
jacket.

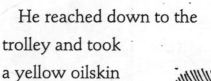

And now
for the Float
Coat.

Sellotaped
inside the
coat were
three empty
milk cartons,
four balloons,
half a dozen
tennis balls and
a beige-coloured
loofah from the
bathroom.

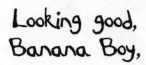

Looking good, Banana Boy,

said Hooey as Twig pulled on the bright yellow coat.

"It's quite comfy, actually," said Twig. "But the question is, does it work?"

"Put it this way," said Will, "if they'd had these on the *Titanic*, things would have turned out very differently."

35

There was a scraping sound
coming from the doorway and
Hooey turned to see Dingbat
slowly dragging a green welly boot
into the room.

"Ah, my trusty assistant," said
Will. "Fetch the other one,
Dingbat!"

With an enthusiastic
yelp, Dingbat bolted out
of the room and returned a
few seconds later, tail first,
dragging the second boot
behind him.

"Having a bit of trouble there, boy?" asked Hooey as Dingbat struggled towards them with the boot. Hooey bent down to try and pick it up, but it seemed to be stuck to the floor.

"Wow," said Hooey. "These boots are hard to move."

"Maybe they're magical boots!" said Twig. "Maybe my magical wimple-hat is casting a magical spell on them!"

Bending over to point at one of them, he chanted,

Boot, boot, stop your trick. Let young Hooey ... up you pick.

"Twig, that's terrible," said Hooey, finally managing to lift up the boot and carry it into the middle of the room.

"Worked though, didn't it?" said Twig. "They don't call me Mister Magic for nothing."

"Mr Muppet, you mean," said Hooey. "What did you put in these boots, Will? Concrete?"

"Certainly did," said Will. **"They're my Gravity Boots."** He pointed to a diagram on the wall. "I made a mould of my leg from Plaster of Paris, stuck it in the boot and then poured concrete round the outside. When the concrete set, I just smashed up the Plaster of Paris and, hey presto! Gravity Boots."

"Genius," said Hooey, as Dingbat helped him drag the other boot into the centre of the room. "All set, Twig?"

"All set for what?"

"For my Windy Weather Wear Test, of course," said Will.

Hooey looked at him. "Should I take cover?"

"Best to be on the safe side," said Will. "Just stand behind the fan and you'll be fine."

"Oh, great," said Twig. "What about me?"

"You're the safest one in the room," said Hooey. "You've got all the protective gear on, remember?"

"How could I forget?" said Twig.

39

Will pushed the button and there was
a faint hum which grew louder as the fan
picked up speed. At first there was only
a gentle breeze which cooled the air and
ruffled the curtains. Then, as the fan blades
turned faster, the socks on Twig's ears began
to lift and flap in the wind.

"I'm going to increase the power a bit now," said Will, raising his voice so he could be heard over the noise of the fan. "Remember: head down and wimple to the wind."

Twig leaned forward purposefully.

"OK," he said.

WARDROBES AND WIMPLES

The speed of the fan increased. Twig pointed his wimple to the wind. His coat flew out behind him and the cardboard flaps in his trousers buckled upwards, as if trying to escape through his pants.

"HOLD STEADY, TWIG!" shouted Will. "BELIEVE IN YOUR BOOTS!"

Dingbat's fur was blowing back as if he was leaning out of a car window on the motorway.

Will looked at his clipboard, then at
his watch, and ticked the box that said:
30 SECONDS AT FULL POWER. Then
he pulled a black metal box from beneath
the bed, turned to the next page and wrote
TURBO-CHARGER at the top.

Nice,
said Hooey as
he watched the red
light blinking on and off.

"If I've done my calculations
right," said Will, "this should

increase the fan's speed by a factor of ten."

"Won't that be dangerous?" asked Hooey,
plugging it into the fan.

"**I hope so**," said Will. "Otherwise I've
just wasted two weeks' pocket money."

Want to press
the button?

he asked,
handing the turbo-charger to Hooey.

"I thought you'd never ask,"
said Hooey.

For a moment, nothing happened.
Then, with a hum like a swarm of
bees, the speed of the fan increased and
the floor began to shake. The curtains
billowed up against the ceiling and Will's
"World's Best Inventor" mug hurtled off the
shelf and bounced across the carpet. Twig
squealed. He rose up into a vertical position,
his mouth open, and his cheeks and trousers
flapping in the wind.

"Aunt Em!" he cried. "Aunt Em,
I'm coming home!"

Then, as the fan howled up to maximum speed, Twig flew out of his gravity boots, somersaulted back across the room and smashed into the wardrobe. There was a loud bang, a flash of light and then the only sounds were the gentle hum of the fan slowing down and the honk of a car alarm a few streets away.

Now THAT was windy,

said Hooey,
plucking one of
Will's drawings
off his face.

Will picked up his
clipboard and wrote:
MAKE GRAVITY
BOOTS
HEAVIER.

"Where's
Twig?" asked Hooey.

At that moment, the wardrobe door
swung open and Twig staggered out.
His trousers were torn, his
hair was blown back and he

was staring around the room as if he had
woken from a dream. He turned to look
at the wardrobe, then peered down at
Dingbat, whose fur was all fluffed up around
his head.

"*Am I in Narnia?*" he whispered.

Hooey took Twig by the arm and led him
to a comfy cushion.

Top
testing,
Twig,

he said,
removing Twig's
Wind-Cutting
Wimple. "But
maybe you should
just take it easy
for a bit."

He opened the window
and hooked the Wind-Cutting
Wimple over the window catch
using the bungee cord.

50

"There," he said.
"That's a bit tidier."
Outside, the light was fading.
Shirts flapped on washing lines and
seagulls circled high above the ocean, their
feathers bright against the darkening sky.
"Storm's on its way," said Hooey.
"Thank goodness for Gravity Boots."

THANK GOODNESS FOR GRAVITY BOOTS, repeated Will, writing it down. "Nice slogan. We could use that."

"How about: GRAVITY BOOTS. THEY'LL SMASH YOU INTO A WARDROBE," said Twig.

Will shook his head. "I like the first one better," he said.

Just then, Dingbat, whose fur was still ruffed round his neck, caught sight of his reflection in the mirror. He let out a yelp of surprise and tore across the room and into the smallest hiding place he could find. Unfortunately, the smallest hiding place he could find was Twig's Wind-Cutting Wimple, which happened to still be attached to the elastic bungee cord that Hooey had hooked around the window catch.

The more Dingbat tried to squeeze himself into the Wimple, the more the bungee cord stretched.

Unhook it, Hooey,

said Will nervously.

"Unhook what?" said Hooey.

He turned to see Dingbat clawing his way across the carpet, the wimple wedged on his head and the elastic bungee cord humming like a telegraph wire.

"Oh," he said.

"*That.*"

With a loud **THWANG**, the bungee cord flung Dingbat across the room and out of the window like a stone from a slingshot.

cried Hooey, running
to the window just in
time to see Dingbat sail
away over the rooftops.

"Is he all right?" asked Twig.

"Of course he isn't," said Hooey. "He just got wanged out of the window at a hundred miles an hour!"

Will checked his clipboard.

"I'd say ninety-five, tops."

"Never mind what speed he was going," said Hooey.

We have to find him NOW!

56

They hurried downstairs and peered out into the storm. The wind was howling around the house and rain ran down the road like a river.

"**That is some serious weather out there,**" said Twig.

"Quick test," said Will, taking a tissue from his pocket. As he held it outside the door, the wind whipped it away as if it was attached to an elastic band.

"That's windy all right," said Hooey, turning to look at Twig. "Lucky you're wearing **Will's Wet and Windy Weather Gear.**"

"Yeah, I'm all about the luck," said Twig.

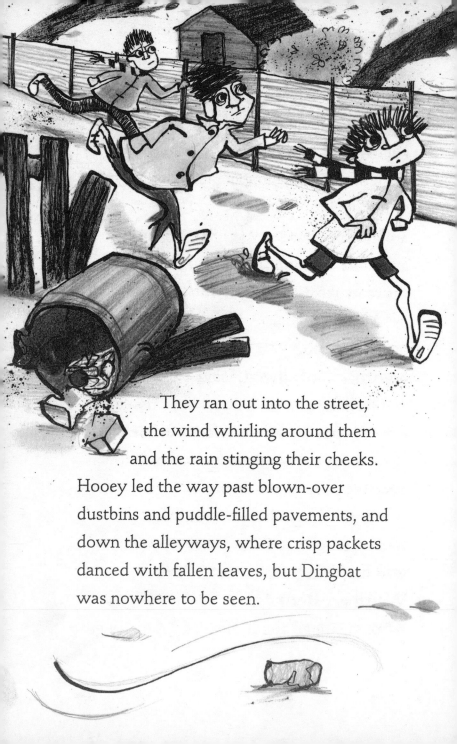

They ran out into the street,
the wind whirling around them
and the rain stinging their cheeks.
Hooey led the way past blown-over
dustbins and puddle-filled pavements, and
down the alleyways, where crisp packets
danced with fallen leaves, but Dingbat
was nowhere to be seen.

"It's a mystery," said Hooey.

"A bit like the mystery of why they put that weird yellow stuff on bananas," said Twig. "I mean, hello, people? Haven't you heard of shrink-wrap?"

For a moment they stood in silence with the rain pounding the pavements all around them, listening to the wind and wondering whether they should just give up and go home. It was Will who spoke first, although it was hard to hear him above the howling wind.

"What we need is more energy," he said. "Some kind of special substance that our bodies can convert into brainwaves, which will then help us solve the problem."

"You're talking about sweets, aren't you?" said Hooey.

"Of course," said Will. "Anyone got any money?"

"Hello, Mr Danson," said Twig as the door to the sweet shop dinged open.

Have you got anything for a pound?

"I thought you had two pounds," said Will.

"I need to save a pound for the way home," said Twig. "In case I need extra brainwaves."

"You'll need more than a pound," said Hooey.

"Don't listen to him," said Twig, turning to Mr Danson. "He's had a terrible shock."

Mr Danson raised an eyebrow.

"What kind of shock?"

"The kind you get when your dog gets wanged out of a window," said Twig.

"I see," said Mr Danson, running his finger along the jars of sweets. "In that case, may I recommend a mixture of Toffee Bon-Bons, Cola Bottles and Sherbet Pips?"

"Good call," said Hooey. "How about a couple of Pineapple Chunks in there too?"

Oh, mwah!

cried Mr Danson, kissing the tips of his fingers and reaching for the jar. "Yes, indeed! Spoken like a true confectioner!"

He shook the sweets into a paper bag, mixed them up and gave them to Twig, who handed him a two-pound coin. Mr Danson bowed, opened the till and gave Twig his change.

"For when you return," he said. Then he looked at Hooey with a wistful expression.

"I know what it is like to lose something precious," he said. "When I was in France a few years ago, a lady gave me the most delicious ice cream I had ever tasted.

She told me it was made from sherry and bananas, but when I got home and tried to make it, it tasted terrible. The secret is lost for ever."

"Maybe not," said Will. "Did she tell you the ingredients in French?"

Mais oui, said Mr Danson. "She said it was 'Banane, sherry'."

"I think I might be able to help you there," said Will, reaching into Mr Danson's freezer and pulling out a tub of Ben & Jerry's.

"What do you reckon?"

Mr Danson stared at it.

"Banane, sherry," he said. "Ben & Jerry. Hmmm..."

He took off the lid, dipped his finger and popped a lump of ice cream into his mouth. Then he closed his eyes and murmured, "**Oh, oui, c'est formidable!**"

"I think he likes it!" said Twig.

"You," said Mr Danson, opening his eyes and smiling, "are a genius."

Twig blushed. "Well, I don't know about that..."

"**He means Will,**" said Hooey.

"Right, good, brilliant," said Twig.

"You know, there was actually another time when I lost something," said Mr Danson dreamily, digging out another lump of ice cream. "I remember I was at school at the time. One minute it was there, the next minute it was gone."

"Same with Twig's thoughts," said Hooey, looking at his watch. "Sorry, Mr Danson, but I think we're going to have to go, or we'll be late for school."

"Of course, off you go, boys!" said Mr Danson.

He sighed as he watched them run down the street, thinking about what he had lost all those years ago. Then he remembered the ice cream and smiled, and helped himself to an extra big dollop.

Don't get blown away!

CHAMSIES AND
BEZZIE-BATS

"Settle *down*, children," said Miss Troutson
as a small squirrel blew out of the tree and
smacked against the window.

"Ooh, that's gotta hurt," said Ricky, as the
squirrel squeaked and slid down the glass.

"Never seen a squirrel do that before,"
said Wayne, looking up from his copy of
Tractors Weekly.

"My dog did it earlier," said Hooey.

"What, threw a squirrel against a window?"

"No, got blown out of one."

Hooey watched the squirrel run back towards the tree and hoped that Dingbat had landed somewhere safe.

"They should make Getting Blown Through Stuff an event for Sports Day," said Twig. "It'd make a nice change from all that running about."

"Yes, because that wouldn't be stupid at all," said Samantha.

"Samantha says I'm not stupid at all," whispered Twig. "Maybe there *is* romance in the air. Maybe my horoscope was right."

"If by *right* you mean *wrong*, then, yes, it was," said Hooey.

"We'll see," said Twig. "I like a challenge."

"Who's whispering?" said Miss Troutson. "I can hear whispering."

"My nan thought she heard whispering once," said Ricky. "Turns out she just needed her ears syringed."

Miss Troutson glared at him.

Ricky Mears, what have I said about being a silly boy?

"I didn't know you were one," said Ricky.

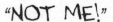

"NOT ME!"
shouted Miss Troutson.
"You! *You're* the silly boy!"

"But I was only—"

"No!"

"But my nan—"

"Shush!"

"With her ears—"

"Be quiet now! Not another word. I mean it, Ricky. No. More. Silliness."

"Yeah, well, good luck with that," said Wayne.

Suddenly Basbo stood up.

Lucky chamsy!

he shouted.

"Azzee godda leafy fing? I wann seeyit wivva four ovvum annatt."

"Barry, please," said Miss Troutson wearily. "Can we just get on?"

Basbo clenched his fists and scowled.

"Leafy fing wivva foruvvumm annatt!"

I think he means a four-leaf clover,

explained Samantha. "Four-leaf clovers are supposed to bring good luck, and Wayne said 'Good luck with that'. I think Barry thought that by 'that' he meant a four-leaf clover."

"Good grief," said Miss Troutson. "Are you sure?"

71

"Asssitt, yerr," said Basbo. "Forleef clovey-wam. Noice, innit. Lucky chamsy."

Miss Troutson sighed. "Barry, I'm sure if anyone finds a four-leaf clover, you will be the first to know. In the meantime, I want you all to pay attention."

She turned to the whiteboard.

This is a diagram of the water cycle,

she said.

"My nan has one of them," whispered Ricky. *"She rides it to the swimming pool on a Wednesday."*

"I mean it, Ricky," said Miss Troutson. "Not another word."

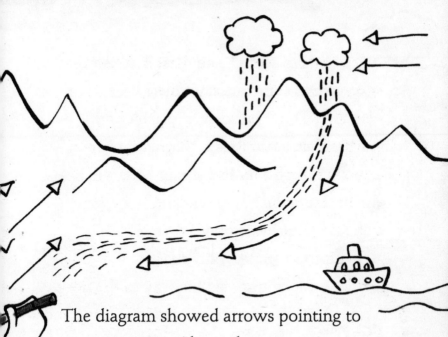

The diagram showed arrows pointing to some mountains. Above the mountains, more arrows pointed to some clouds, some rain, some rivers and back to the sea again.

"Bit of a *weather* theme going on today, Twig," said Hooey.

"Yeah, *whether* or not Basbo's going to kill me," said Twig. "It's not fair. I'm doing my best to cram a few extra facts into my head and all he wants to do is **shove it down the toilet**."

"I'm sorry," said Miss Troutson. "Did someone say toilet?"

"Don't be sorry, it wasn't your fault," said Ricky. "Or, was it?"

"Right, that's it," said Miss Troutson.

"But I was only—"

"Outside. NOW!"

Ricky fumbled his way to the door. Miss Troutson now glared at Twig and said, "Well? Was it you?"

"Me?" Twig pointed to himself.

"Yes, you."

"I think Twig was actually trying to give you an example of the water cycle," said Hooey quickly. "The rain comes down and fills the reservoirs.

We drink some of it and some of it goes down the toilet, which eventually goes back to the sea where it evaporates and makes clouds, which then rain in the reservoirs and the whole thing happens all over again. In a cycle. A water cycle, if you will."

For a moment the room went silent. Miss Troutson stared. Somewhere down the corridor, an infant coughed. Then, to Hooey's relief, Miss Troutson's face softened.

"Is that true?" she asked. "Is that what you were going to say?"

"**Yes, it is!**" said Twig. "And correct me if I'm wrong, but I think Florence Nightingale invented it."

Looking out of the window, Hooey could see Ricky Mears standing in the playground, shielding his face from the leaves and bits of paper being blown about by the wind. He was about to tell Miss Troutson that he thought Ricky might have misunderstood the word "outside" when the bell rang for break time. Miss Troutson grabbed her coffee cup, shouted "COATS!" and rushed out of the classroom towards the staffroom.

Goats?

said Wayne. "Where?"

"She said 'coats', you doughnut," said Yasmin.

"That makes more sense," said Wayne.

"I expect all that stuff about the water cycle made her thirsty," said Twig.

"Teachers are always thirsty," said Wayne. "My dad says they spend all their time in the pub, laughing and eating crisps and falling over."

"Probably just reminds them of school," said Hooey.

In the playground, the wind was so strong that most of the reception class had been blown over and were lying on their backs, staring at the sky.

"That's weird," said Hooey as an infant walked past with diamond patterns on his face. "Maybe they're doing a project on tattoos or something."

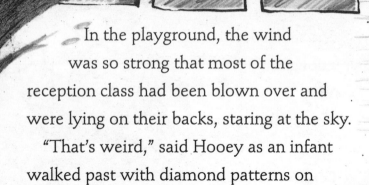

Two more infants ran past, holding their coats open and leaping into the air. The wind picked them up, hurled them across the playground and slammed them into the fence. As they bounced back onto the tarmac, they shrieked with laughter and ran back across the playground with the criss-cross diamond shapes of the fence imprinted on their faces.

"That answers that one," said Hooey.

"Coming over," said Twig as three more infants flew past and crunched into the side of the shed.

An extra-strong gust
of wind caught the
fourth one and
blew him over the shed roof.
There was a moment's silence,
followed by a faint **splash**.

"CONSERVATION
AREA!"

shouted Hooey. "Quickly!"

They found Basbo standing in front of the gate with a baseball bat.

"No go inna Constipation Area," he said. "Constipation Area dayn-juss, innit."

"But someone just fell in the pond," said Twig.

"Go way," said Basbo, "else I'll bash yer eddin wivva bat."

"What's going on here?" demanded Miss Troutson, striding around the corner. She tapped the end of Basbo's baseball bat. "And what's all this?"

Izza bezzy-bat,

said Basbo.

"Well, I can see that," said Miss Troutson. "But the question is, what are you doing with it?"

"Stoppina peoples a cumminninna Constipation Area. Juss like a-Missy Troutser say."

"I didn't say you had to go around hitting people with a baseball bat, Barry," said Miss Troutson. "I just said make sure no one goes in the Conservation Area."

Basbo thought for a moment, handed the baseball bat to Miss Troutson, then reached inside his jacket and pulled out a rounders bat.

Miss Troutson nodded. "Much better," she said.

"But, Miss Troutson,
Bertie Milsom just
fell in the pond,"
said Twig.

Don't be
ridiculous,

said Miss Troutson.
"Bertie Milsom knows as
well as I do that people aren't
allowed to fall in the pond
without permission."

"He didn't mean to," said
Hooey. "He just sort of flew
over the shed."

At that moment there was
a rustling sound and Bertie
Milsom emerged from
the undergrowth.

Hello, Miss Troutsy,

he said as the playground fence twanged with the sound of more infants landing on it. "**'Tis windy.**"

"Never mind the weather forecast, young man," said Miss Troutson. "What on earth do you think you're doing in there?"

"I ran out of sky, I did," said Bertie. "And then I did fall and I did land in the pond."

He smiled sweetly and put his thumb in his mouth.

Bertie go sleepy-time now.

"Oh, no, you don't," said Miss Troutson, unlatching the gate and hauling Bertie to his feet. "Go and stand in the hall and think about what you have done. And when you have thought about it, go and tell Mr Croft. Do you understand, young man?"

"Yessir, Missa Troutsy," said Bertie and set off towards the hall. Hooey could hear him practising:

Oh, hello, Mr Croftyman. I did run out of sky. I did fall in the pond. I did see a dog...

Hooey looked at Twig. "Did he say 'dog'?"
Twig nodded. "I think he did."
"Right," said Hooey.

A BOOT FOR BASBO

Leaving Miss Troutson heading towards the
playground shouting, "Stop being silly! Stop
it right now!", Hooey and Twig dodged past
Basbo, leapt over the fence and ran towards
the pond.

Arrrgh!

shouted Basbo. "No goan inna
Constipation Area!"

"Don't panic," said Hooey, as Basbo jumped over the gate. "Just act natural."

Twig nodded and cleared his throat. "*Lovely day, lovely day,*" he sang in a squeaky voice.

"Maybe not *that* natural, Twig," said Hooey.

Just then, Basbo growled and raised the baseball bat above his head. Twig let out a whimper and ran behind Hooey.

"If he asks, just tell him I've gone to play football with Florence Whats-er-face."

"I don't think that's going to work," said Hooey. He smiled at Basbo and said, "Me and my friend Twig here were just looking for my dog."

Basbo lowered his bat and stared at Hooey.

Dog?

Hooey nodded. "Dingbat's gone missing and Bertie said something about seeing a dog in here."

Basbo pointed his bat at the water.
"Dog inna pond?"
"Well..."
"Not dog inna pond," said Basbo. "Frog inna pond. Dog inna kennel."

"Well, this one isn't," said Twig, peering over Hooey's shoulder. "This one got himself wanged out of a window."

Basbo pointed the bat at Twig.

"Twiggler tryna be funny?"

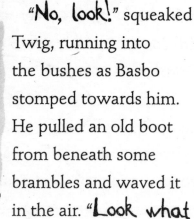

"No, look!" squeaked Twig, running into the bushes as Basbo stomped towards him. He pulled an old boot from beneath some brambles and waved it in the air. "Look what I found!" he cried. "It's for you!"

"Bootster not Basbo's," grunted Basbo.

"Twig, what are you doing?" hissed Hooey. "He's not Cinderella."

"I know that," said Twig. "But you know what I think? I think this shoe once belonged to a **horse**. And one day the horse came clippety-clopping through here and saw the pond and went, 'Oh, no! A pond! Uh-oh! Whoopsie!' Then he stepped out of the way and one of his shoes fell off. And it's been lying here ever since, just waiting for some lucky person to come along and find it. And that lucky person is ... YOU!"

Twig walked over and shoved the boot under Basbo's nose.

This is your Lucky Horseshoe. And I was the one who found it for you!

Basbo took the boot.
He sniffed it, then
frowned so hard that
his eyebrows met in
the middle.

"How hossy do vemmup?"

"Beg pardon?" said Twig.

"I wantsa know," said Basbo,
pointing to his shoes, "how hossy
duzza laces up."

Twig shrugged. "Maybe he's got a special
horse friend who does them up for him."

"You fink I stupid, dunnoo,"
growled Basbo. "You fink I fink
a dog livinna pond anna
hossy doo nuppizz shoesies.
Well evbod knows hossy izza
wearina slip-ons, innit. So
now eyes-a bashin' yer eddin."

"No, wait," said Twig, dropping to his

knees. "I'm sure I saw a four-leaf clover down here somewhere."

He stuck his head beneath the bushes and scrabbled around in the dirt. Apart from a piece of string, a marble and a rusty old ring pull there was nothing to be found.

Twig scrambled to his feet. But just then a strong gust of wind lifted the lid off the compost bin and cracked him on the back of the head with it.

"Unngh!" he said, falling forwards into Basbo's arms. "Fmmmf!".

"Werrrg!" said Basbo, stumbling backwards.

Flerrb!

For a moment the two of them teetered on the edge of the pond, Basbo windmilling his arms around and Twig clinging desperately to his jacket. Then another gust of wind lifted them both off their feet and dumped them in the middle of the pond.

shouted
Basbo as he surfaced.

Twig popped
up next to
him, the boot
perched neatly
on his head.

"Y'frinkin' framberton!"
Basbo yelled, grabbing the
boot and hurling it into the bushes.
"You lucky chamsies no
workin', not nowsy not
never. You lucky chamsies
big pile of—"
    "Look!" shouted Hooey,
pointing towards the playground.
    "The trees are on the move!"
        Basbo and Twig turned to see the
        branches of the two oak trees
            trembling and moving
            from side to side.

"It's like that film *The Railway Children*," said Twig. "We should probably take off our petticoats and wave them."

"No time for that," said Hooey. "We've got to warn them!"

"Kill im first," said Basbo, pointing at Twig.

"No time for that either," said Hooey. "You'll have to kill him later."

Basbo nodded.

Killoo later.

They leapt
over the fence
and ran into the
playground just
in time to see a
flying infant knock
Miss Troutson to the floor.

"For goodness' *sake*," she
said, pushing the small
boy off and struggling to
her feet. "How many times have I told
you to stop this *nonsense*?"

"Thix timeth I think,"
lisped the boy. "Thix
or theven."

"**Then kindly do
as you are told**," said
Miss Troutson as another infant
shot past her, hitting the fence and
bouncing back across the playground.

99

"Excuse me, Miss Troutson," interrupted Hooey, "but I think the trees are on the move."

"They're not trees, they're infants," said Miss Troutson. "Can't you tell the difference?"

"I don't mean *them*," said Hooey, his shorts flapping in the wind. "I mean *those*." He pointed at the two oak trees, which were swaying and creaking like a pair of old doors.

Trees wann come say hello,

said Basbo. "Thass not good nooz."

Before Miss Troutson could reply, a whistle blew and Hooey turned to see the headteacher, Mr Croft, standing in the middle of the playground. He was wearing a crash helmet.

"Teachers, children and flying infants!"

he shouted, struggling to be heard over the sound of the wind. "**Storms are no place for silliness!** Stop your shenanigans and go back to your classrooms! And Miss Troutson's class, report to me for storm duties immediately!"

"Storm duties?" said Twig. "What are they?"

"Same as normal duties, but with extra hundred-mile-an-hour winds," said Hooey.

Shweet,

said Twig. "Sign me up!"

TREE TIME

"Sandbag duty?" said Twig. "*Sandbag* duty?"

"You can say it as many times as you like," said Hooey, taking a sandbag from the shed, "but it doesn't change the fact we've still got to do it."

"Why couldn't we be on Getting Tea and Biscuits For the Teachers duty? Or the Inside Where It's Warm Making Sure the Infants Don't Panic duty?"

"Because you volunteered us for this one, that's why."

"I don't think I did," frowned Twig.

"OK. So when you stuck your hand up and went, 'Ooh, pick me, Sir,' you weren't actually volunteering, then?"

"I thought he said 'handbag duty'."

"Twig, why would he say handbag duty? I don't even know what that is."

"I expect you have to go around fetching people's handbags," said Twig. "In case they want to put on a bit of lippy or something."

"Twig, shut up and fetch another handbag. I mean a sandbag."

"See?" said Twig sulkily. "An easy mistake." He picked up a sandbag, ran across the playground and dropped it by the entrance to the toilets.

"I don't see why we have to do this anyway. It's not even raining."

"I know, but Mr Croft says it might do later. And if it does, the rain always comes down the steps and floods the toilets. That's what happened last year, remember?"

Twig looked doubtful. "I thought it was just one of the infants who didn't make it in time."

"It was pouring out of the door."

"I know, but have you seen those infants at the water fountain? They drink like little guppies."

"Never mind that, Twig. Let's get a pile from the shed and then we can build it up from the inside before the rain comes. That way we won't get wet."

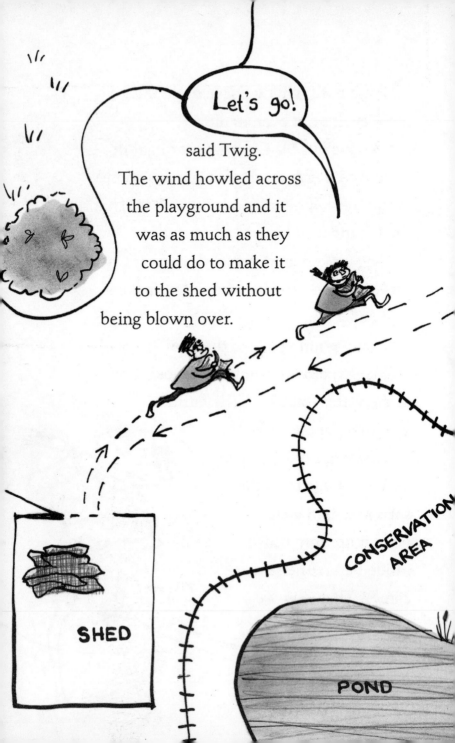

TOILET BLOCK

BIG OAK TREE

But they worked fast, and before long there was a neat pile of sandbags in the middle of the toilet block.

They were about to start stacking them in the doorway when Ricky Mears poked his head around the door.

"I've got
good news
and bad news,"
he said.
"The bad news is,
Mr Croft just gave Basbo a detention
for dripping water all over the carpet.
Now Basbo's gone crazy and he's coming
this way."

"Uh-oh," said Twig. "What's the good
news?"

"The good news is, Basbo says you've
brought him bad luck and unless you've got
him a lucky charm, he's going to kill you.
Wait. That's not good news at all. Oh well.
See ya!"

Twig took out his horoscope, crumpled it into a ball and threw it away in disgust. Then his face lit up.

"Hooey, quick!" he shouted. "Get me a bully gun!"

Hooey frowned. "Would that be a gun for shooting bullies, or a gun used by bullies to shoot people?"

"Ummm…"

"Because we don't have either."

Twig buried his face in his hands.

I am so dead. Unless. Unless…

"A-ha!" Twig picked up the sandbags
and started piling them up in the doorway.

"Quick! Help me build a wall before he
gets here!"

"But—"

"No time to argue!" said Twig, stacking
one on top of the other. "Just slide them
across to me!"

Hooey began sliding sandbags across
the floor. There weren't enough to fill the
doorway, so while Twig was busy stacking,
he ran out to fetch some more from the
shed. He had only managed a few steps
before the wind tore the door off its hinges,
sending it cartwheeling
across the playground.

Hooey heard a creaking, groaning sound. The brick circle surrounding one of the oak trees appeared to be wobbling, its edges moving up and down like a wave as the tree lurched sideways. Then, as he watched, the bricks popped out of the circle one by one, flying into the air and smashing into pieces on the playground.

Uh-oh,

said Hooey.

Arriving back at the toilets, he was
puzzled to hear Twig's voice saying:
"Pass me another, he'll be here in
a minute!"

Wondering where the extra sandbags
were coming from, Hooey ran around the
corner and saw Twig with his back to him,
busily stacking sandbags in the entrance to
the corridor.

One more
should do it,
said Twig, holding
out his hand as another
sandbag slid across the floor.

"Umm, Twig," said Hooey.
"There's probably something you
ought to know."

"The only thing I need to know," said Twig, chuckling to himself, "is that Basbo won't get through this lot in a million years."

He turned around and the smile slowly disappeared from his face as he found himself staring at Basbo.

"Thank you very much," whispered Twig, as Basbo slid the final sandbag across the floor towards him.

"Yew got meeda lucky chamsy?" asked Basbo, getting to his feet and brushing the sand from his fingers.

"Nope," said Twig.

Basbo sighed, rolled up his sleeves and cracked his knuckles.

he said.

At that moment there was a groaning,
splintering sound, the roof of the toilet block
exploded and several tons of solid
oak came crashing through
the ceiling.

As the dust settled, Hooey noticed that
the toilet roof had disappeared and the wall
had become a pile of bricks with an oak tree
on top. A chunk of plasterboard rose slowly
from the ground to reveal Twig
underneath, covered from head to
toe in white plaster dust.

"Wow," he said. "That must have been some punch."

He caught sight of his white reflection in the mirror and pressed his hands to his face in horror.

Oh no!

he cried. "I'm a ghost! I am actually a ghost!"

He turned to Hooey and his lower lip wobbled. "Hooey, dear friend, I know you probably can't hear me. But if there's some way I can make you understand, I want you to tell my nana I'm sorry for putting bubble bath down the toilet. They really ought to put a warning on that stuff."

119

"**Shut up, you numpty,**" said Hooey. "I can hear you and you're not a ghost. Although, to be honest, I have seen you look better."

Twig put his thumbs up. "Not a ghost. **Shweet.**"

He glanced around the broken toilet block. "I see the sandbags worked, then."

The top of the tree had smashed into the toilet cubicles. The branches were resting against the far wall and the door of the nearest toilet was hanging off its hinges.

"*Twig,*" Hooey whispered, "*did you hear that?*"

Twig put his head on one side and listened. "*Is anybody there?*" he whispered. "*Give one knock for yes and two knocks for no.*"

From somewhere inside the cubicle, they heard a whimper.

"Sounds like someone's on the loo," said Twig. "That tree must've really helped 'em do the business."

"Where's Basbo?" asked Hooey.

He looked at Twig, then at the toilet cubicle, then back at Twig.

They ran to the cubicle and tried to push the door open, but something was in the way.

"We'll have to pull it," said Hooey. "Are you ready? One, two ... three!"

There was a splintering sound as they both heaved, then the door came off its hinges and sent them sprawling back across the floor. Pushing himself free of the door, Hooey saw Basbo. His bottom was wedged in the toilet bowl and his arms and legs stuck up in the air.

"Maybe we could just leave him there," suggested Twig. He looked at Hooey's expression. "But that would be wrong."

Big bam bish-bash,

said Basbo as
they pulled him out.
"**Big bam bish-
bash bang
Bazzer-onna
bonce.**"

"Just think of it as
a new experience," said Hooey.
"After all, it's not every day a tree tries to
take your head off in a toilet."

"Talking of which," said Twig nervously,
"we should probably go before he tries
taking mine off."

"Bazzer no take Twig's head off," said Basbo. "Twig bring Bazzer lucky chamsy."

"Eh?" said Twig.

"Yerr, izza lucky rabbit's foot," said Basbo. He pointed to a smudge of mud on his right cheek. "Lucky rabbit come along annee smash Bazzer inna face. Bazzer fall inna toilet anna tree izz missin' im, see? Twig bring Bazzer lucky chamsy and save Bazzer's life."

He grabbed Twig by the ears, kissed him on the forehead and then stomped away up the corridor.

"What was that about?" asked Twig.

Hooey picked up Twig's horoscope from the floor and read:

> **"Your natural charm will bring good luck to someone special and maybe even a touch of romance."**

He grinned. "Maybe you just needed to set your sights a bit lower."

"Ha, ha, very funny," said Twig.
"I reckon he must have got clonked on the
head by one of those branches. I mean, all
that stuff about a lucky rabbit smashing him
in the face and saving him from the tree.
I haven't heard anything that weird since my
nan put whisky on her cereal and accused
the milkman of being a weird milky wizard."

"Maybe he was," said Hooey. "Spending
all day with yogurts can't be healthy.
Although on second thoughts it
does actually sound quite healthy."

"Unlike that," said Twig,
pointing to the toilet cubicle.

Hooey listened and
heard the same faint
whimpering sound
that they had
heard before.

Is there anybody there?

whispered Twig.

"Don't start that again," said Hooey.

"Maybe Basbo went back in there," suggested Twig.

"Why would he do that?"

"The shock, you know. Being hit by a massive tree and all that. Must do wonders for your digestion."

"No way is that Basbo," said Hooey. "It sounds more like ... more like..."

127

Before he
could finish his sentence, there
was a scrabbling sound and then something
very dusty and bedraggled emerged from
the gap beneath the door.

At the front was a silver, pointy hat with
two socks hanging down like ears. And at
the back was a waggy tail that thumped the
floor and sent up puffs of plaster dust like
little clouds of happiness.

"Dingbat!" cried Hooey, getting down
on his knees as Dingbat skidded across the
floor and leapt yelping and slobbering into
his arms.

"Twig," Hooey said,
holding Dingbat at arms length
and looking at the socks hanging down from
the sides of his face, "I think we've found
our lucky charm."

SAUCERS AND SUNSHINE

"So when Bertie Milsom said he'd seen a dog in the sky," said Twig as they walked home along the seafront, "and Basbo said he'd been smashed in the face by a rabbit, they were both actually talking about Dingbat?"

"I guess so," said Hooey as Dingbat barked and ran after a seagull. "When he got wanged out the window, the wind must have taken him over the rooftops and into the oak tree. And when the oak tree came through the roof, Dingbat came through with it, smashing Basbo in the face and knocking him down the toilet. That's why he had a paw mark on his cheek. I expect the last thing he saw when the tree came through the roof was Dingbat with the socks flapping around his head and his foot stuck out in front of him."

"No wonder he looked surprised," said Twig.

132

"Stunned, more like," said Hooey. "Which you would be if you thought a giant rabbit had just fallen through the roof and kicked you in the face."

He looked around at the overturned dustbins and broken branches, and the grey skies clearing to blue.

"It's hard to believe there was ever a storm," he said as the sun came out and warmed their faces. "Although having a massive tree in your toilet might be a bit of a clue."

"Unless you're a dog," said Twig as Dingbat gave up on the seagull and chased an old crisp packet instead. "In which case, a massive tree *is* a toilet."

"Good point," said Hooey. "You see?" He tapped Twig on the side of the head. "You've got plenty of useful facts in there after all."

"And here's another one for you," said Twig, stopping outside the sweet shop. "I've got a magic pound in my pocket that will change itself into a couple of Crunchies when I place it on the counter."

Hooey grinned. "Now *there's* some magic I'd like to see."

When they opened the door, Mr Danson was up a stepladder, hanging Sherbet Flying Saucers from a sign that read:

"Hello, boys," he said. "Bob's Bakery is all very well, but can you buy Sherbet Flying Saucers from him? No, you cannot."

He climbed down from his stepladder and they all looked at the sign for a few moments.

"It's a very nice sign," said Hooey.

"Kind of you to say so," replied Mr Danson, smiling proudly. "**I made it myself.**"

"No way," said Twig. "What are those yellow bits?"

"Sherbet Lemons," said Mr Danson. "I stepped on a couple by mistake and thought it would be a shame to waste them. So I decided to give it an extra sherbety theme."

"I think it works," said Twig. "It would definitely make me want to buy them."

Mr Danson smiled some more and went behind the counter.

"So what can I get you then, hmm? Let me guess ... half a dozen Sherbet Flying Saucers?"

"No, thanks, they taste like cardboard," said Twig. "I'll take two Crunchies, please."

For a moment Mr Danson looked disappointed, but then he remembered that a sale was a sale and took two Crunchies from the display that he had polished earlier, just in case.

"That'll be a pound, please," he said. "It's a pleasure doing business with you."

Twig put his
hand in his pocket
and searched
around for a bit.
He put his other
hand in his other
pocket and searched
a bit more. Then
he put both hands
in both pockets
and searched all over again.

"What's up, Twig?"
asked Hooey.

I think I've lost
my pound,

said Twig.

He emptied his pockets onto the counter.
There was no sign of the pound, only a
piece of string, a marble and a rusty old
ring-pull.

138

"I've lost it," said Twig, "I've definitely lost it."

"*No, you haven't,*" whispered Mr Danson, his lower lip quivering as he stared at the counter. "You've *found* it. You've definitely *found it.*"

As the afternoon sun streamed through the window, he reached out, took the marble and held it up to the light. Hooey could see a twist of blue running through its centre, like a tiny strip of sky.

"Umm, Mr Danson," said Twig, clearing his throat, "I don't think that's a pound." He lowered his voice. "I actually think it's a *marble*."

Mr Danson shook his head and smiled.

"This is not just a marble. This is *my* marble. Don't you see? This is what I tried to tell you about earlier. It was my favourite marble when I was a boy and it must have fallen out of my pocket when I was walking across the fields to school."

"But I found it in the conservation area," said Twig.

"Which I'm guessing used to be a field," said Hooey.

"Exactly," said Mr Danson. "I thought that I would never see it again. But now you have brought it back to me and I couldn't be happier!"

"I could," said Twig. "If I still had my pound."

"What you have brought me is worth more than any pound, said Mr Danson. "And to prove it, here are your Crunchies, and a little something extra."

Producing two very large paper bags from beneath the counter, he took down every jar on the shelf and put a spoonful of sweets from each into the two bags. Then he put a couple of Sherbet Flying Saucers on the top.

"There you go, boys," he said.

Enjoy!

"**Wow, thanks, Mr Danson,**" said
Hooey. He turned to Twig and grinned.
"Looks like your horoscope came true after
all," he said. "Today your life will be—"

"**Sher-weet!**" said Twig.

They closed the door behind them and
Mr Danson watched
them walk down
the road, clutching
their paper bags
and laughing.

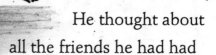

                He thought about
        all the friends he had had
    when he was at school all those years
ago, and all the sweets, and all the laughter.

He picked up the marble and held it up to the light once more.

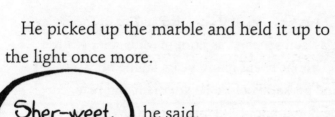

Sher-weet, he said.

Then he smiled, put the marble in his pocket, and helped himself to a Sherbet Flying Saucer.

STEVE VOAKE (also author of the Daisy Dawson series) was born in Midsomer Norton, where he spent many years falling off walls, bikes and go-karts before he got older and realized he didn't bounce like he used to. When he was Headteacher of Kilmersdon School he tried to convince children that falling off walls, bikes and go-karts wasn't such a good idea, but no one really believed him. He now enjoys writing the Hooey Higgins stories and hasn't fallen off anything for over a week.

EMMA DODSON has always been inspired by silly stories and loves drawing scruffy little animals and children. She sometimes writes and illustrates her own silly stories – including *Badly Drawn Dog* and *Speckle the Spider*. As well as drawing and painting, Emma makes disgusting things for film and TV. If you've ever seen anyone on telly get a bucket of poo thrown on them or step in a pile of sick you can be fairly sure that she was responsible for making it. Emma also teaches Illustration at the University of Westminster, where she gets to talk about more sensible things.